THE KING OF SPACE

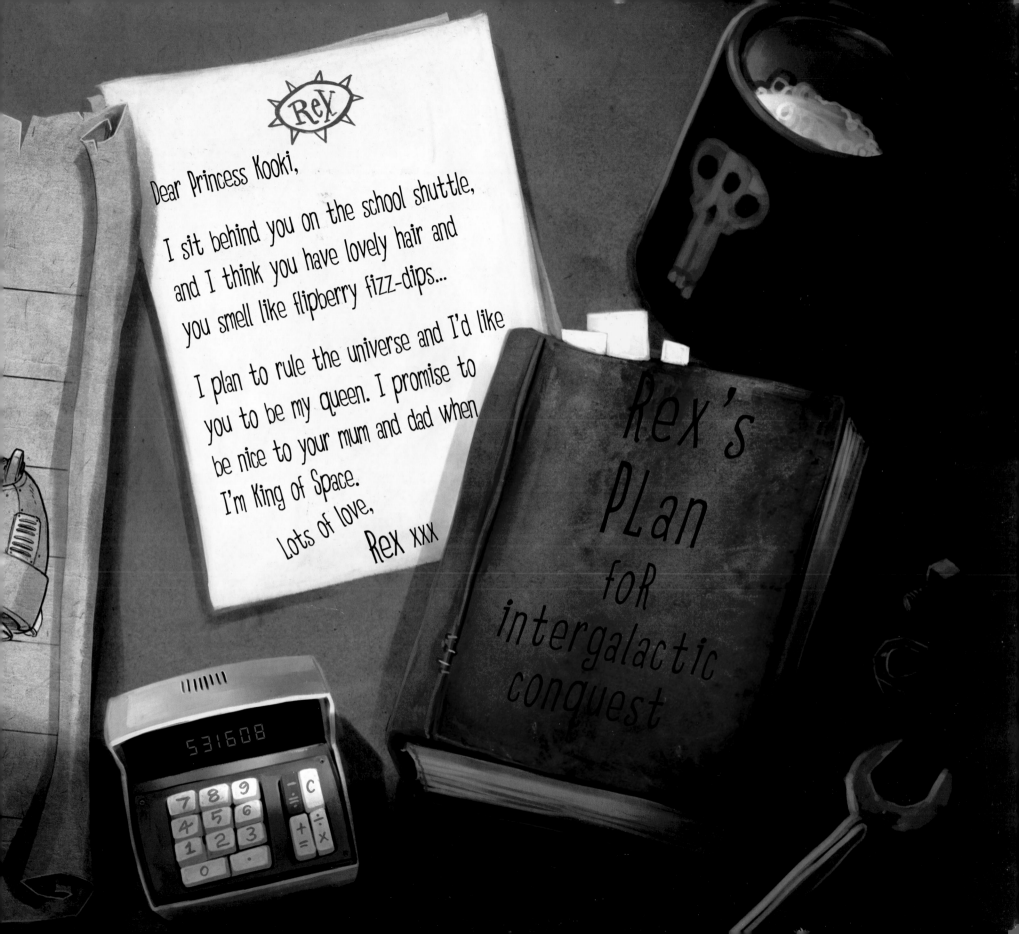

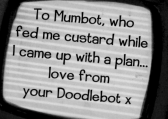

To Mumbot, who
fed me custard while
I came up with a plan...
love from
your Doodlebot x

A TEMPLAR BOOK

First published in the UK in 2013
by Templar Publishing
This softback edition published in 2013 by
Templar Publishing, an imprint of
The Templar Company Limited,
Deepdene Lodge, Deepdene Avenue,
Dorking, Surrey, RH5 4AT, UK
www.templarco.co.uk

Copyright © 2013 by Jonny Duddle

First softback edition

All rights reserved

ISBN 978-1-84877-227-4

Edited by Libby Hamilton

Printed in China

THE KING OF SPACE

by
Jonny Duddle

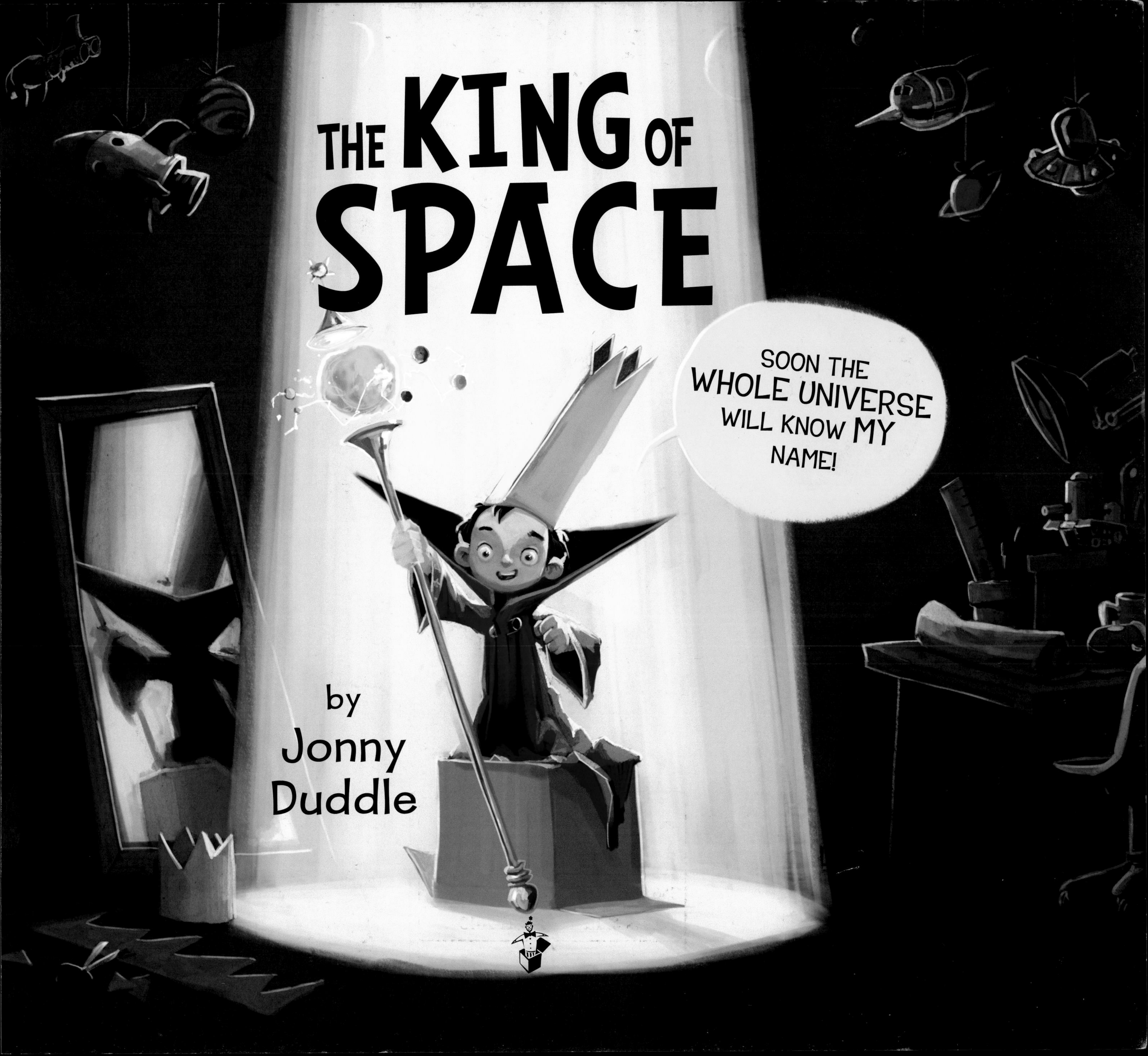

Greetings Earthlings! My name is Rex and I live on a small moon in the Gamma Quadrant, on my mum and dad's moog farm. I may look little, but I have BIG plans...

Mum and Dad say I have too much energy, so they have to keep me busy.

But on this particular night, I was too busy to clean my room.

I'd just thought up my BIGGEST and BESTEST PLAN EVER!

Annoyingly, I couldn't get going straight away because the next day I had to go to Mini Galactic Citizen School.

I'M GOING TO FLY SPACE FREIGHTERS. VROOOOOM!

ERM... IT'D BE REALLY NICE TO FIX DRAINS LIKE MY DAD.

I JUST WANNA MAKE COMPUTER GAMES, DUDE!

YES, MA'AM. I'M TRAINING TO BE A SPACE MARINE, MA'AM!

WELL, MISS BRAIN...

I'VE DEVELOPED A CLEVER PLAN.

Rex's Plan

A PLAN TO TAKE ME FROM THIS LOWLY CLASSROOM TO THE FURTHEST REACHES OF SPACE!

I WILL BE THE KING OF SPACE!

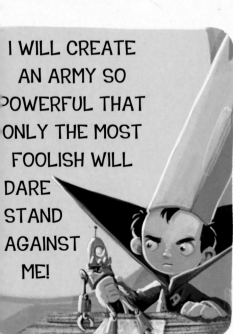
I WILL CREATE AN ARMY SO POWERFUL THAT ONLY THE MOST FOOLISH WILL DARE STAND AGAINST ME!

I WILL CRUSH PLANETS AND SQUISH SOLAR SYSTEMS!

SOON THE WHOLE UNIVERSE WILL KNOW MY NAME...

For homework that night, Miss Brain asked us to each build a robot that could do something helpful.

Miss Brain said she was very impressed with everybody else's robots...

Blip's spaceship-washbot...

Xarg's toast-o-matic (with net)...

Zorick's lawnmower-machine...

and even Glob's drain-unblocking-droid.

Miss Brain asked my mum and dad to come into school.

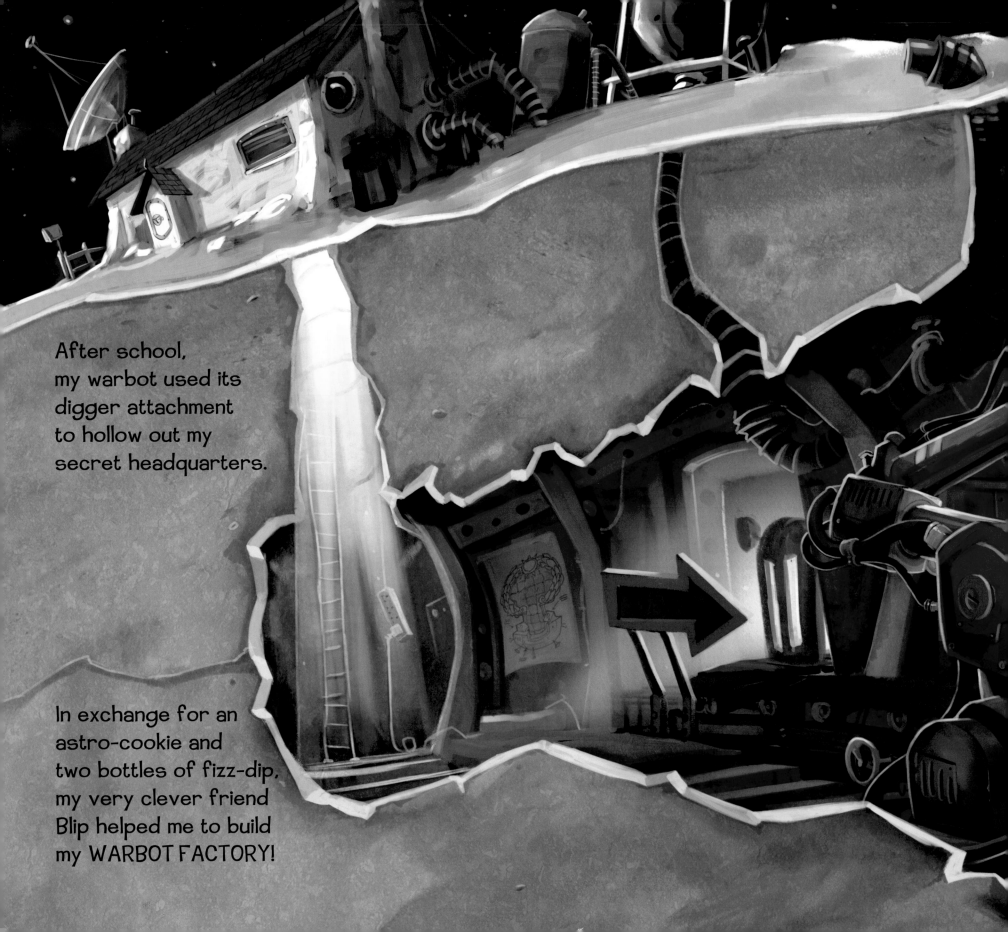

After school,
my warbot used its
digger attachment
to hollow out my
secret headquarters.

In exchange for an
astro-cookie and
two bottles of fizz-dip,
my very clever friend
Blip helped me to build
my WARBOT FACTORY!

Blip said he wouldn't tell anyone about it, as long as I promised to only make nice, friendly robots.

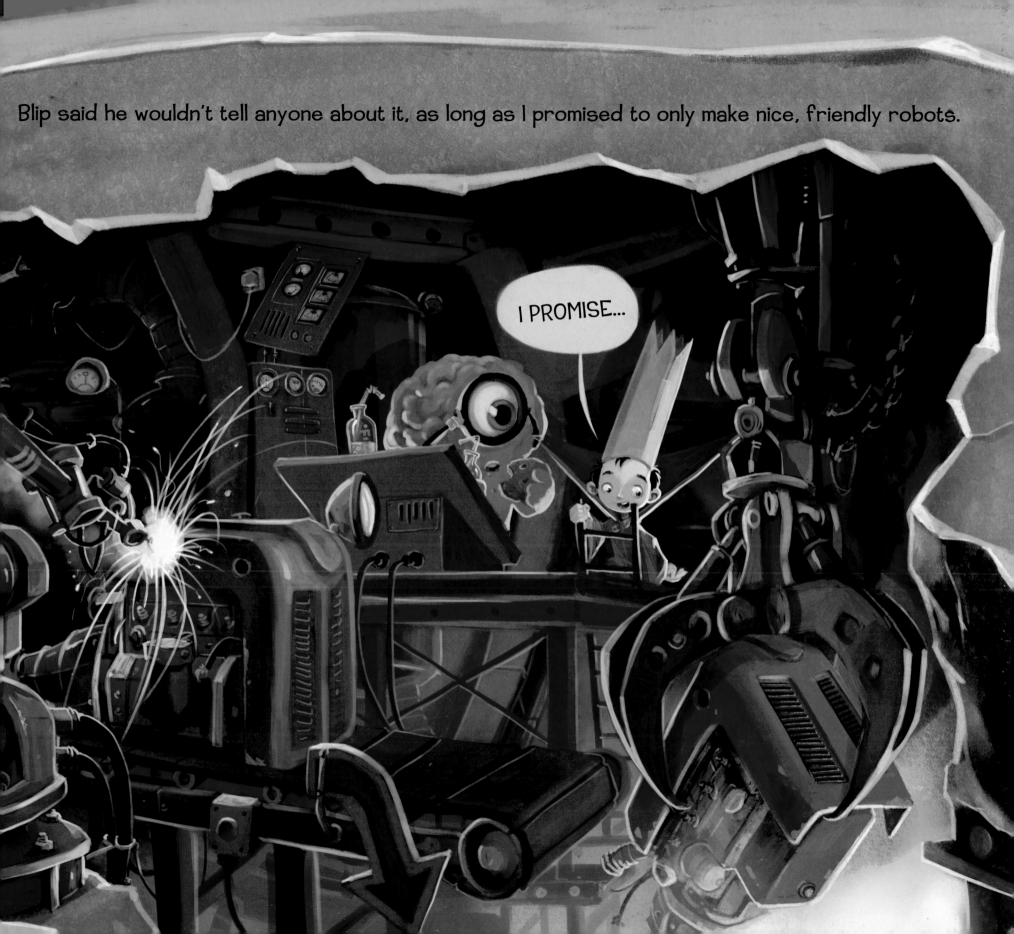

Blip turned out to be very good at making all kinds of machines,
so I told him that, when I became King of Space, he would be rewarded.

MY VERY OWN PLANET?

REEEEEALLY?

YES.

AND I COULD DO WHATEVER I LIKE THERE?

UM...

YES.

I COULD STAY UP LATE AND WATCH TV AND EAT **LOADS** OF CHOCOLATE?

ON YOUR PLANET, YOU'D BE **ALL-POWERFUL!**

WOW!

WOULD I STILL HAVE TO TIDY MY ROOM?

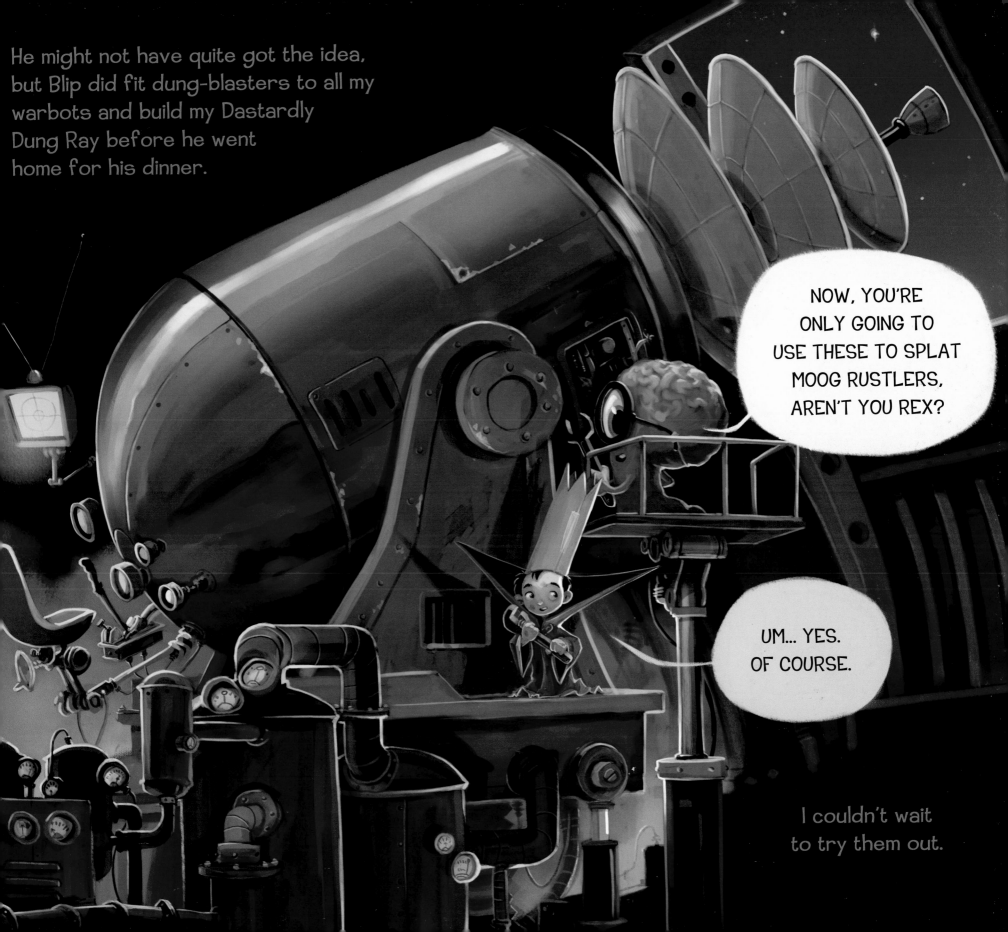

It turned out that, while I'd been away, my worker droids had finished building my throne room.

So I decided it was time for my CORONATION!

I handed out some invitations at school, making everyone promise that they wouldn't tell their mums and dads.

Blip made a clever machine that could transmit live TV images, so everyone in the universe had to watch my coronation ceremony whether they liked it or not.

I NOW CROWN MYSELF THE KING OF SPACE!

CLAP NOW!

I gave a party bag to everyone who clapped a lot.

Unfortunately, my coronation (and dung-blasting) had caught the attention of Emperor Bob and his Galactic Alliance.

I tried to sneak past Mum and Dad to get the choco goo. There was lots of great stuff on the news about my warbots taking over the universe and Princess Kooki being held hostage.

But when I went outside, something wasn't right...

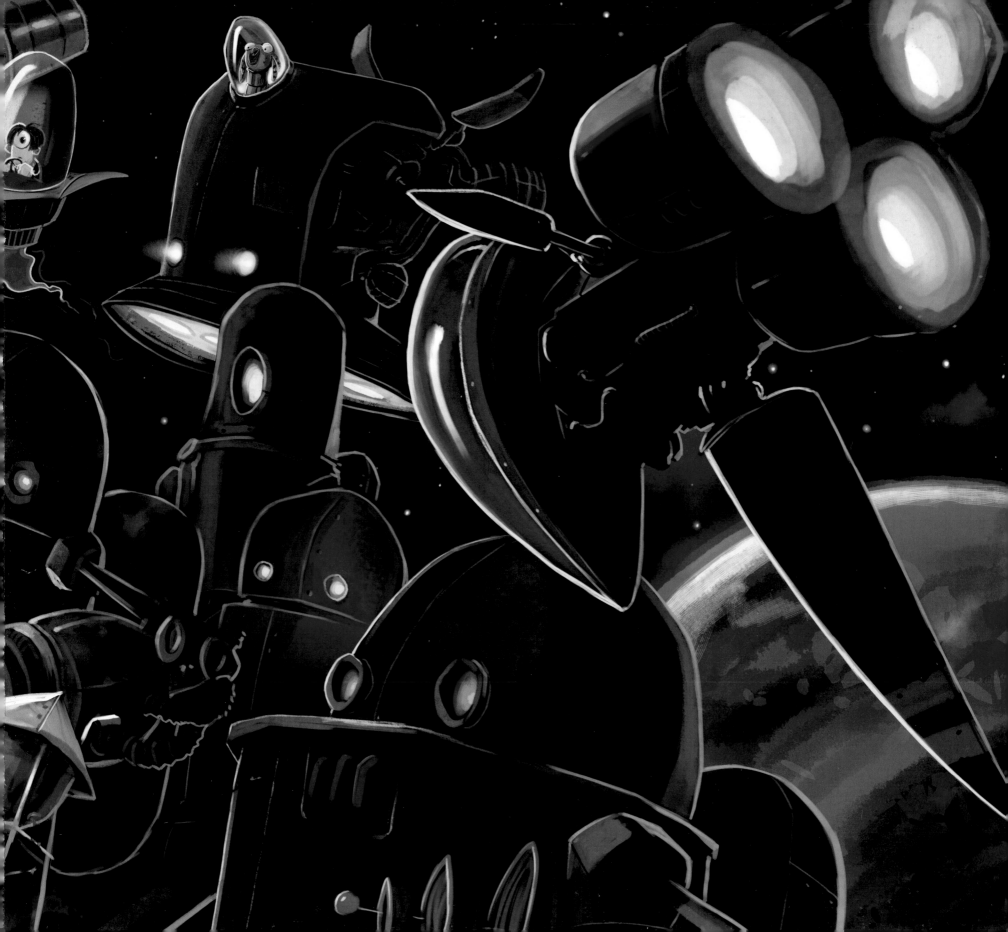

I ran inside and slammed the door.

WHAT'S WRONG, REX?

I... ER... UM... THEY... ERM...

COME ON, HONEYBUN, TELL US!

WELL, THE GALACTIC ALLIANCE ARE OUTSIDE AND THEY'RE REALLY CROSS BECAUSE I INVADED THEIR PLANETS, KIDNAPPED PRINCESS KOOKI AND TOLD THEM I WAS...

THE KING OF SPACE.

THE WHAT?

THE KING OF SPACE.

AND I REALLY AM!

Then I told Mum and Dad everything I'd been up to.
STARTED WITH MY BIGGEST PLAN EVER...
REX
BLIMEY.
...AND NOW I DON'T WANT TO PLAY ANYMORE!
YOU LEAVE THIS TO ME...

Mum said she was going outside to have a word with the Galactic Alliance.

NOW, YOU LISTEN HERE! REX IS A VERY TIRED LITTLE BOY. HE DOESN'T WANT TO PLAY ANYMORE, SO I THINK IT'S TIME YOU **ALL** WENT HOME!

OH, AND PRINCESS KOOKI SAYS SHE **DOESN'T** WANT TO STAY FOR CHOCO-GOO, SO COULD YOUR MAJESTY POP DOWN AND TAKE HER BACK WITH YOU?

Luckily, even the Galactic Alliance can't say no to Mum, so they all went home.
Then Dad made me some hot milk, helped me brush my teeth
and read me a bedtime story.

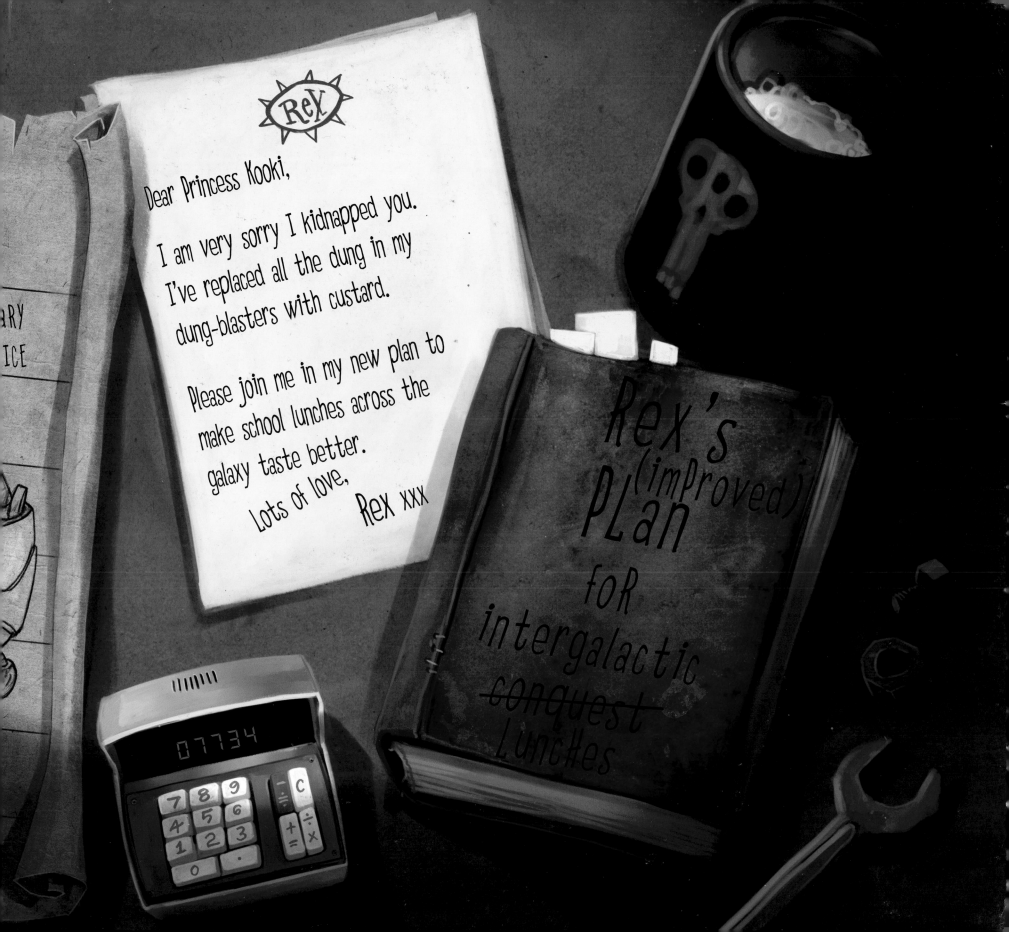

GREETINGS EARTHLINGS!

MAKE SURE YOU CHECK OUT
THESE OTHER BEST-SELLING ADVENTURES
CREATED BY **JONNY DUDDLE**...

The Pirate-Cruncher

AND WATERSTONES
CHILDREN'S BOOK PRIZE WINNER

The Pirates Next Door